PRESENTED BY

Mary Lowell Downing

1996

SMYTHE GAMBRELL
LIBRARY

WESTMINSTER SCHOOLS

FIRST APPLE

FIRST APPLE

by Ching Yeung Russell

illustrated by Christopher Zhong-Yuan Zhang

BOYDS MILLS PRESS

Special thanks to my husband, Phillip Russell,
who helped me with this project; and,
of course, to my editor, Karen Klockner,
who patiently guided me — C.Y.R.

Text copyright © 1994 by Christina Ching Yeung Russell
Illustrations copyright © 1994 by Boyds Mills Press
All rights reserved

Published by Caroline House
Boyds Mills Press, Inc.
A Highlights Company
815 Church Street
Honesdale, Pennsylvania 18431
Printed in the United States of America

Publisher Cataloging-in-Publication Data
Russell, Ching Yeung.
First apple / by Ching Yeung Russell ; illustrated by
Christopher Zhong-Yuan Zhang.—1st ed.
[128]p. : ill. ; cm.
Summary : Living in China during the late 1940s, a young girl works to save
enough money to buy an apple and give it to her grandmother for her birthday.
She and her grandmother have never tasted an apple.
ISBN 1-56397-206-9
1. China—Social conditions—1912-1949—Juvenile fiction.
[China—Social conditions—1912-1949—Fiction.]
I. Zhang, Christopher Zhong-Yuan, ill. II. Title.
[F]—dc20   1994
Library of Congress Catalog Card Number 93-74360

First edition, 1994
The text of this book is set in 14-point Galliard.
Distributed by St. Martin's Press

10 9 8 7 6 5 4 3 2 1

To Jonathan and Jeremy,
with all my love,

and

To my Ah Pau,
whom I will always remember

— C.Y.R.

CHAPTER 1

"*A* fantastic show is going to be performed! A fantastic show is going to be performed!" I began to yell as loud as I could to be heard above the rain as I walked out of my house to the quiet, empty plaza. Ah Mei and Ah Pui dashed to their houses to get ready.

"A good show is about to take place! It's the best show ever! Don't miss it! If you do, you'll regret it for the rest of your life!" I walked to the end of the plaza and kept advertising our show. I was the one who could yell the loudest and exaggerate the best.

Heads popped out of doorways. The kids all asked, "Who's going to be in it?"

"Ah Mei, Ah Pui, and I—the most popular stars you have ever seen!"

"How much for admission?"

"It's a Sunday afternoon special—only five peanuts or thirty kernels of corn or thirty incense sticks! The cheapest but most spectacular opera show in the whole wide world!"

"I don't have peanuts. How about a raw sweet potato?" six-year-old Ping asked. He was Ah Pui's brother.

"Sure! Anything! Anything we can eat is welcome!"

The ones who didn't have food dashed into the rain, trying to get the incense sticks from the burners that were placed next to every family's front door for the earth god. The sudden activity startled the chickens that lay under-

neath the eaves, hiding their heads beneath their wings to avoid getting wet.

We lived in Chan Village in the small town of Tai Kong. Our village was located at the foot of Ford Hill, next to the temple. My uncle said that our village was in a good location because we were only one block from Tai Gai, the main street. We were two blocks from the ferry and a couple of miles from Tai Kong Primary School. But I didn't care much about the location. All I cared about was whether there was someone to play with! There were fifteen boys and girls about my age, all cousins, whose last names were Chan. I was the only one named Yeung, but when I played or argued or fought with them, I forgot that I was Yeung and they were Chan.

I only yelled back and forth along the plaza three or four times and then ran back home. I had goose bumps all over and was sneezing. My pants and back were wet from the rain.

Ah Mei returned from her house with three long scarves, and Ah Pui brought three of her baby sister's blankets. We went inside my room and wrapped the baby blankets around our waists as skirts. We didn't own skirts ourselves. Only the people who lived in big cities, like Canton, did. We tied the long scarves around our waists to keep the "skirts" from falling down.

Then I got a calligraphy brush and dipped it into my ink box to paint Ah Mei's eyebrows. Ah Mei painted mine and Ah Pui's. I sneaked three empty *lai see* money pockets from Ah Pau's worship table. We quickly licked the money pockets and wet the red dye. Then we rubbed them on our cheeks for rouge and pressed them between our lips for lipstick. After we finished our makeup, Ah Mei and Ah Pui looked funny, like clowns, but I didn't tell them. They might want to start all over, especially Ah Mei. She always liked everything to be perfect. Even her two long pigtails were always neat and shiny, unlike mine.

I wanted our show to be finished before my family came home from visiting, so I hurried into the living room. The audience was already waiting since we didn't close our front doors in the daytime. There were about nine kids, aged four to eight. They were anxious to hand in their food and incense sticks to Ah Pui, who was the one to collect the admissions.

While Ah Pui was busy, Ah Mei and I wiped our dirty feet with our hands. (We all went barefoot, except for a couple of days during Chinese New Year.) Then we climbed up on my cousin Kee's bed. His bed was in the living room, and there was a long worship table at the end of the room. The bed was on one side of the room, and a round, red folding table served as a dining table on the other side. I lowered the mosquito net so that it completely enclosed us. We pretended that the net was the theater curtain and the bed was our stage. Ah Mei moved Kee's pillow and thin cotton quilt to the corner of the bed so they would not be in our way.

"What did we get?" I asked Ah Pui after she climbed onto the bed. She had two handfuls of "admissions." Ah Pui was eight, one year younger than I. Her hair was cut short, above her ears, like half a coconut shell. She was not as tricky as I was. She never plopped any "admissions" into her mouth when she was collecting them.

"Not much," she said, turning all of it over to me.

There was one small raw sweet potato, a handful of cooked corn kernels that we usually ate one by one as a snack, and a big bundle of incense sticks that I couldn't hold in one hand. But there were no peanuts.

Ah Pui said, "There are thirty-four corn kernels. How can we divide them?"

Ah Mei and I both were in third grade, but she was ten, one year older than I. Her math grade was always 100. She said without thinking, "Each of us will have eleven."

"How about the other one?" I asked.

"Divide it by three, too." So she used her fingers to cut it into three tiny pieces. It was fair. We giggled and popped the corn kernels into our mouths, while the kids in the audience sat on the clay tile floor in front of Kee's bed, raising their heads eagerly to watch us through the gauzelike mosquito net. I heard Ah Ping yell, "When are you going to start the show?"

"Wait!" I held my nose tight to keep from sneezing while I still had corn kernels in my mouth. Then I hurriedly swallowed the food and said, "How can we sing with empty stomachs?"

The kids must have thought Ah Ping was rude to ask that question because several of them booed.

The sweet potato was small and round. We couldn't use our hands to break it, and I didn't want to go to the kitchen to cut it with a cleaver.

"I have an idea," I said. I wiped the potato on my clothes, then bit off a piece, and handed the rest to Ah Mei.

Ah Mei rubbed the potato on her sleeve to wipe off my germs. Then she took a bite and handed the rest to Ah Pui.

But the potato slipped from Ah Pui's hand. She moved quickly toward the edge of the bed to pick it up.

Suddenly she screamed, "Ohhhh!"

CHAPTER 2

Before we knew what was happening, the piece of board Ah Pui was standing on went down like a seesaw, and the other side of it shot up in the air! Our beds were made out of several pieces of board put together, with only a woven sea grass mat on top of them.

"Are you all right?" I asked, helping Ah Pui get up. But I couldn't keep from laughing.

Everybody was laughing. Ah Pui laughed, too, massaging her rear end at the same time. The audience had something to entertain them at last and temporarily forgot the show. We could finish eating the potato in peace.

The show finally started. As always, I was the announcer, so I opened the "curtain." Ah Mei and Ah Pui hooked the mosquito net on both sides of the bed the way we did during the day-time when nobody was sleeping. The audience was quiet now. They were expecting the fantastic show I had advertised. I cleared my throat and announced, "Today we are going to perform *The Moon Lady*."

"No! We've seen it before!" Ah Ping protested.

"Yes! Do another one!" eight-year-old Ah Sum said.

"*The Old Man Moved the Mountain*—how about that?"

"No! We saw it last time!" they replied together.

"Well . . ." I tried to think of the opera that

Ah Pau had told me about many times. "How about *The Cowboy and the Weaving Lady?*"

"Good!" they all agreed as they mumbled to each other.

"But who is going to be the cowboy?" Ah Mei seemed worried. "I don't want to be a boy."

"I don't, either," Ah Pui said.

"It doesn't matter. I just gave them a new title so they won't think we are tricking them," I whispered.

"Why don't *you* be the cowboy? You are the tallest," Ah Mei suggested.

"No, I don't want to," I whispered. "We can have two ladies and one maid. They won't know the difference."

"Okay," Ah Mei said. So we started the show. Ah Pui was always the maid because she was the youngest and never protested. All she did was pretend to sweep the floor or dust or take care of the mistress. Ah Mei and I had the main roles, but we didn't know how to sing. It didn't matter; our audience didn't know any

better. As long as we made sounds and moved our hands around, they were happy. Since Ah Mei and I didn't know any words to the opera, we began to sing *yee yee ya ya,* imitating the high-pitched voices with up-and-down, long-and-short sounds.

Suddenly I shivered and felt chilled all over. Ah Mei noticed, and she sang, "Are — you — cold ?" She braced both arms on her chest.

I sang, "I — feel — cold — suddenly."

Then she sang, "Your — clothes — are — still — damp. You — will — get — sick — and — won't — be — able — to — play." Then she covered her eyes and pretended she was crying.

I sang, "I — am — strong — and — I — will — not — get — sick. — If — I — get — sick — nobody — will — play — with — me." Then I made my hands as limber as I could and covered my heart with them to show it was a broken heart.

"I — think — you'd — better — "

At that moment, I noticed that Ah Mei's voice sounded like a chicken squawking when its head was being cut off, and all the veins in her neck stuck out. I burst out laughing. Ah Mei and Ah Pui saw me laughing, and they laughed, too, even though they didn't know what I was laughing about. I was afraid the audience would notice, so I quickly closed the "curtain" for the end of the scene, and we kept on laughing so hard that I almost wet my pants!

I knew the audience really enjoyed our first scene because Ah Ping told the other kids to be quiet as soon as I reopened the "curtain." We continued our show.

Because Ah Pui was the servant, she knelt down in front of us, pretending to offer tea. Then Ah Mei began to sing. I noticed that she was reciting some prose from our reading book. All she did was sing the words up and down, short and long. Since Ah Mei was doing that, I decided to sing some Chinese classical poems that my uncle had taught me. I sang Li Po's "Thoughts on a Quiet Night": "The — moon — shines — brightly — on — my — bed. — I

— raise — my — head — and — gaze — at — the — bright — round — moon. — I — lower — my — head — and — think — about — my — homeland." I pointed to the moon and pretended that I was very sad about missing my hometown.

I heard Ah Mei sing, "Your — face — looks — as — if — you — are — going — to — be — hanged."

I was about to laugh when suddenly Kee and Ah Man dashed in, all wet. Ah Kee demanded, "Hey! Get off my bed!"

Ah Mei and Ah Pui were scared to death. They jumped off the bed at once, while the audience begged, "Please, Kee, they haven't finished yet."

I was not scared of Kee, and I knew he was not really that mean. He was eleven, and in fifth grade. We were first cousins because my mother and Kee's father were sister and brother. Ah Mei, Ah Pui, and the others were my second cousins.

I continued to recite another classical poem.

It was T'ao Ch'ien's "Back to Farm and Garden." Kee realized what I was doing, and he announced loudly, "She is reciting poems! She is cheating you!"

"Yeah! Ask them to return whatever you gave them!" Ah Man shouted. Ah Man was Ah Mei's older brother, also a fifth grader, and Kee's best friend. But Kee was tall and skinny, and Ah Man was short and big-boned.

When our loyal audience knew that I was not really singing opera, Ah Ping demanded, "I want my potato back!"

"I want my corn back!"

"I want my incense sticks back!"

I yelled back to them, "It's too late unless you get it from the bathroom!"

"Yuck!"

I tried to bargain with them, but Ah Ping and Ah Sum jumped on the "stage" and tried to grab the incense sticks. I held onto them firmly, refusing to let go. Before I knew it, someone was jumping up and down on the bed. Suddenly the mosquito net fell on top of us, and we looked like trapped animals. We screamed and yelled and tried to get out of the net. We had completely forgotten about the food and the incense sticks.

Bang!

Someone slammed the door to get our attention. Then I heard Ah Pau shout, "Are you going to tear down my house, huh?"

CHAPTER 3

I woke up. It was dark, except for the small flame of the kerosene lamp. My throat hurt, my right ear hurt, and I was hot. I started to cough. Ah Pau heard me coughing and tossing around. She parted the mosquito net and touched my forehead. "Your fever is still high. I am going to give you a cool bath." Ah Pau sounded very worried.

"Am I going to die, Ah Pau?" I asked, half asleep and half awake.

"Oh, no! Ah Pau is keeping a close eye on you."

I needed to ask her more questions, but I didn't want to talk. I just wanted to sleep. I let Ah Pau give me a cool sponge bath while I was half asleep.

When I woke up the next morning, Ah Pau had fallen asleep on the chair beside my bed. Whenever she heard me, she awoke.

"Why didn't you sleep in your bed, Ah Pau?" I asked. Her bed was just about three feet away from mine. We shared a room.

Ah Pau mumbled something that I didn't hear well. She hooked both sides of the net for me and asked, "How do you feel?"

"I don't know. My head and ear still hurt."

After she pulled the thin cotton quilt over my shoulders, Ah Pau hurriedly poured a bowl of herbal medicine and carefully put it in front of me. She said, "If your fever is still high after you drink this, I am going to take you to see the doctor. You've had a high fever for two days now."

"I don't want to drink that; it tastes bitter."

"For your own sake—even if it *is* bitter—you still have to drink it."

"I don't want to. I drank half a bowl yesterday, and it still didn't make me well."

"You have to take it at least a couple of times before it affects you."

"And it almost made me throw up."

"I have raisins ready for you. All you do is *glug glug*, and it will go right down to your stomach." Ah Pau convinced me. She was my mother's mother, about seventy years old. She was small—not much taller than I. She yawned several times. Then I noticed that she hadn't changed her black *tong cheong sam*. She always wore black like the other old ladies, and the small bun of gray hair at the back of her head was still pinned up. So I asked, "You didn't go to bed last night?"

She didn't answer my question. She only said, "Don't worry, I will catch up on my sleep

later. Here, the medicine is the right tempera-
ture. Take it before I have to heat it up again."

I didn't want Ah Pau to heat up the medicine because she would have to start the clay
stove all over again. She had already stayed up
at least two or three hours in front of the clay
stove to slowly cook the herbal medicine. To
keep the fire going in the stove Ah Pau had to
add pine needles or dried leaves constantly,
since we hardly ever used firewood. Wood was
very expensive. I knew Ah Pau fixed the medicine just for me, so I didn't complain anymore,
even though I was afraid I would throw up.

I took the bowl from her hand. It was half
full of brown liquid. Even before I drank it, I
knew from the smell that it was bitter. But I
would drink it for Ah Pau, so I *glug glug glug*
drank it with one breath. Ah Pau handed
me the raisins. The pharmacy gave them out
with the medicine so we wouldn't drink any
water and dilute the medicine. The raisins were
supposed to make the bad taste go away. I

plopped a handful of raisins into my mouth, but they were tasteless.

The next time I woke up it was very bright, and I was sweating like crazy. Ah Pau was still sitting beside my bed, watching me. She looked tired but happy. She said, "You're sweating. That means you must be getting better."

I pushed myself to sit up and asked, "Why is it so bright?"

"You slept for a long time. School is almost over now," Ah Pau said. She fixed my pillow so I could lean against the wall. I shook my head. It didn't hurt, and my ear and throat did not hurt as much as before.

"I am feeling much better, Ah Pau."

"I knew it." She wiped my face and my neck and helped me change my underclothes. "Next time don't be so silly," she instructed. "When you get wet, change into dry clothes as soon as possible, okay?"

"I will listen to you, Ah Pau." Even though Auntie, Ah So, and Uncle had come in to ask me how I felt, Ah Pau was the only one to stay by my bedside to take care of me. She was always there for me, ever since my parents had left me with her and gone to Hong Kong. I was only five years old then.

My uncle worked in his dry foods grocery store on Tai Gai seven days a week, and he even ate at the store. When I went to school, he was still in bed; when I went to bed, he was still working at his store. Auntie was not in good health. She always coughed, and she had three people to take care of: Uncle, Kee, and Ah So. Ah So, Kee's older sister, was sixteen, and she was busy learning how to cook and embroider. She was preparing to be a wife. And Kee couldn't take care of me; he just bossed me around.

I asked, "Ah Pau, why aren't you afraid that you will get my germs?"

Ah Pau looked into my eyes and simply said, "Because I am your Ah Pau."

It almost made me cry. I tried very hard to hold back my tears as I said, "When I grow up, I'll take very good care of you, too, Ah Pau."

31

"That's very sweet of you." Ah Pau pushed back a strand of my hair and said, "Do you want to sit up in the living room for a while? You've been lying in bed for two days."

"Yes, my back is sore," I said, and Ah Pau helped me take my pillow and thin quilt to the living room so I could lean on the wooden daybed next to the round folding table. I thought Ah Pau would rest, but she said, picking up my dirty clothes, "I'm going to buy some fish fillets and make fish *juk* for you so you can gain back your strength. Are you hungry?"

"Yes!" I liked to eat fish *juk*. It was rice porridge with fish balls.

"I thought so, since your forehead is cooler than before."

"Where *is* everybody?"

"Auntie and Ah So have gone to the farmer's market to try to find a bargain. Kee will be home soon. I'll be back as soon as possible."

Before Ah Pau left, I asked her to hand me my bookbag. As she did so, she said, "Try to rest and don't get up and down a lot. You are not completely well yet."

I promised Ah Pau. After she left, I tore one page from my notebook and drew a picture of myself on the bed. I drew Ah Pau falling asleep on a chair next to my bed and wrote, "Thank you for taking care of me, Ah Pau."

CHAPTER 4

*A*fter school Ah Mei came to visit with her woven bamboo bookbag still in her hand. "Hey, I ran into your Ah Pau. She said your fever is down and you are feeling much better. Are you?"

"Yes, Ah Pau has been staying up to keep an eye on me."

"Hey! What's that?"

"Just a note for my Ah Pau."

Ah Mei read the note and said, "But she doesn't know how to read."

"I know, but I can read it to her. You know what? When I grow up, I will take very, very good care of her, and I will give her a real present, not just a note."

"That's nice. Here, this is for you." Ah Mei handed me a get-well card. It was also made from a piece of notebook paper.

"Whaah, it's neat!" It had a big red apple colored with a bright red crayon on the front.

"Sorry I can't give you a real one."

"I like it. Thank you."

"Do you know why I drew you an apple?"

"Uh-uh."

"Because today we learned where apples grow."

"Oh, where? I've never seen an apple tree!"

"Up north."

"You mean Shanghai? Peking?"

"I guess."

"No wonder they're so expensive here."

"Of course. They need to be shipped all the way down here."

"Do you think apples are expensive in Canton, too?"

"They're probably cheaper than here."

"Why?"

"Because Canton is a big city."

Tai Kong was located about seventy-five miles southeast of Canton, which was the biggest city in south China. The town extended from the foot of Ford Hill to two or three miles away from it. A branch of the Pearl River flowed around the town. I didn't know how many people lived in Tai Kong, but we had only three streets and several short blocks. We didn't have any public transportation in the town, not even bikes. We just walked everywhere barefoot.

It was the 1940s and there were electric lights, but only on Tai Gai. They were not bright at all. Every family still used kerosene lamps. The town had only one primary school, one theater—which was not always open, no library, no hospital, and no fire station. When there was a fire, someone would bang a big gong and yell, "Fire! Fire!" Then all the men would pull their handmade carts with buckets of water and run toward the place that was on fire.

"What does living here have to do with the price?"

"Because they have to ship the apples to Canton, then from Canton ship them here."

"Oh, I see." I looked at the apple on the get-well card and said, "I wonder what an apple tastes like."

"They are *sweet and crunchy!* Don't you remember?"

"Oh yeah." In our first-grade textbook there had been a picture of a bright red apple. It had said, "Apples are sweet and crunchy." Everybody who had gone to first grade would know that.

"But *how* sweet? *How* crunchy?" I wanted to know. The book didn't say clearly.

Ah Mei shrugged her shoulders. "It's clear

to me. Sweet means sweet; crunchy means crunchy."

"Not to me!" I'd always wondered, were they as sweet as mangoes or papayas? Were they sugary like lichee nuts or longans? Were they crunchy like sugarcane? The textbook didn't say anything about that. I said, "It didn't say how, and I don't even know what the inside of an apple looks like!"

"I don't, either."

"If I could try one, *just one,* then I could find out."

Ah Mei teased me, "You are dreaming. You know how expensive apples are."

I didn't answer her. I had something on my mind.

CHAPTER 5

When Ah Pau came back from the market, I gave the thank-you note to her. "What does it say?" she asked, sitting next to me.

"It says, 'Thank you for taking care of me, Ah Pau.'"

"Oh, you are so good." Ah Pau looked at the picture I had drawn. I explained to her, "See, that is me lying on the bed. That's you falling asleep in the chair. You are too tired from taking care of me, Ah Pau."

"You can draw well."

"Are you going to keep it forever, Ah Pau?"

"Of course."

"Ah Pau, am I a good girl?" I jumped at this chance. "I was sick for two days and couldn't go out to play. I drank your herbal medicine even though I was afraid I would throw up. I listened to you and didn't jump up and down. Since I was so good, would you buy me an apple for a reward? It will also give me back my strength."

Ah Pau laughed out loud. "I knew you had something on your mind from the way you talked. But an apple!"

"Yes, I want to find out how it tastes, and I want to see what it looks like inside, too. Would you?"

"I wish I could, Ying. But I could buy a lot of other fruits for the price of just one apple! They are so expensive, I don't even dare to ask the price."

"But you always told me to try to eat *every-*

thing, especially the vegetables I don't like."

"You sure know how to persuade people." Ah Pau laughed. "But you know what? When I was your age, I also dreamed about eating an apple."

"You did?"

"Yes, just about . . . maybe several months older than you are now. I envied my landlord's daughter because she always had apples to eat."

"Did you ever try one?"

Ah Pau shook her head. "Apples are rich people's fruit, not poor people's. You know that your great-grandfather, my father, was a poor rice farmer."

"But how about when you were older?"

"The older I got, the more I realized that it was just a little girl's impossible dream."

"But *everything* is possible. Mrs. Yu said so."

"Well, that may be what she said. But I will be seventy-one years old in about ten more days, and I still haven't been able to eat an apple."

"Whaah! Seventy-one in just ten days?"

"Yes, time flies, doesn't it?"

"Are we planning to have a big feast like other people do when they are seventy-one?"

"Uncle says so, even though I told him not to."

We were going to have a feast! All the aunties in the village would help prepare the big meal. And we would have all the tables in the plaza because the house was not big enough for everyone, including the boys and girls in the village. Besides that, the grandparents would give presents to Ah Pau. Even if they didn't, Uncle and Auntie would give Ah Pau a present.

Ah Pau was always so good to me, I should give her something, too. I had never given her a present on her birthday, but she always gave me a hard-boiled egg and *lai see* money on my birthday. What if I gave her half an apple for her seventy-first birthday present, and I could taste the other half? That way I wouldn't have to wait until I grew up to give her a real gift, and her long-time childhood dream would come true!

CHAPTER 6

*T*he next day I went back to school, and during the last period we had a calligraphy contest. We had to turn in two pages of big characters. I wanted to have mine in on time so I wouldn't be delayed in going to the fruit store to check the price of apples. I did pretty well on the writing. As I was about to finish the last two characters, I suddenly let out a cry. "Aiyah!"

Ng Shing had punched me on my left elbow! My right hand, which was holding the brush, jerked and dashed a big black mark across my paper.

"What's going on?" Mrs. Yu asked. She was grading papers at the back of the classroom.

"Ng Shing hit me and messed up my paper," I said, about to cry. Now the paper would not qualify for the contest.

"Her elbow went across to my side!" Ng Shing defended himself. He was supposed to be in fifth grade, but he was repeating third grade for the second time. He often disturbed the class.

Mrs. Yu, our third-grade homeroom teacher, made Shing share a desk and bench with me because I was the youngest in the class, and she thought I wouldn't mind. She hoped that Ng Shing would behave himself, but Shing used his knife to carve a line in the middle of the desk. If my elbow accidentally crossed to his side, he would punch my elbow without any warning. I wanted Mrs. Yu to change our seats, but Ah

Pau, like other parents, respected the teacher's decision and said, "She has her reasons. All you need to do is be careful and watch your elbow."

So I tried to watch my elbow and not go across to his side when I wrote. But I had been nervous about the contest and I forgot.

Mrs. Yu came over and simply said to Ng Shing, "Be reasonable, Ng Shing." Then she said to me, "Sorry about that. I'll let you start over on another sheet and hand it in to me in the office."

So I was late leaving school. I ran straight to Hing Kee, the biggest fruit store on Tai Gai, to see if there were any apples for sale. There were bananas, with the price written on a piece of cardboard—one cent apiece; persimmons—three cents for big ones, one cent for small ones; star fruits—two cents for one; black sugarcane—one cent for a one-foot piece; Oriental pears—two cents for one; pomegranates—two cents for one; and Chinese grapefruit—fifteen cents for a catty.

There was a lot of fruit, all arranged neatly in

baskets. But there were only four bright red apples stacked at the back of the other fruit, with no price. That meant they were expensive. That's why I had never paid any attention to them. *This* time I wanted to get a closer look at them, but I was afraid. I stood in front of the store, wondering how much it would cost for an apple.

"Hey, young lady, want to buy something?" the fat, bald-headed owner asked.

"I . . . want to know how much an apple costs."

"Sixteen cents."

"For a catty?" I asked innocently. I thought he had misunderstood my question.

His eyes opened wide. "Are you kidding? Sixteen cents for *one!*"

"For *one!* Just for *one?*" I asked. I could hardly believe it! For sixteen cents I could buy sixteen bananas, or sixteen small persimmons, or sixteen feet of sugarcane. Even the most expensive Chinese grapefruit sold for fifteen cents for a whole catty. No wonder Ah Pau didn't even dare ask the price!

"Go home and don't bother me," the fruit store owner said. He waved his hand, motioning me to leave.

As I left the fruit store, I heard a rough, familiar voice behind me. "You want to steal one, huh?" It was Ng Shing.

I ignored him, but he stepped in front of me and shouted, "You wanted to steal!"

"Who says?"

"Me. Why are you standing in front of the fruit store and not buying anything?"

"None of your business!"

"I'll tell on you."

"You are disgusting." I wanted to walk away, but he stopped me. I wished Kee were here.

"If you say I am your boyfriend, I will not tell on you."

I hated him. I would rather let *anyone* be my boyfriend but that bully! That would be much, much worse than his punching me on my elbow.

About two weeks before, Ng Shing had

passed around a drawing of a boy and a girl. They were kissing. Ng Shing's name was under the boy and my name was under the girl. It said, "Ng Shing is going with Yeung Ying."

I was very mad. Who wanted to go with that bully? But the class laughed and started calling me Ng Shing's girl. I cried and reported the drawing to Mrs. Yu, who had six daughters and was pregnant again, hoping for a son.

Mrs. Yu only said, "Just ignore it!" She didn't punish Ng Shing. No wonder we all thought she favored the boys.

"Say that I am your boyfriend," he persisted, "if you don't want me to tell on you."

I couldn't stand it any longer. I dashed around him and ran home, even though I wanted to spit in his face!

CHAPTER 7

*B*ack home, I took my clay piggy bank from underneath my bed, dumped the money out, and counted it. I had only two one-cent bills. I needed fourteen cents more.

"Ah Pau, where is Kee?" Ah Pau was in the courtyard, trying to mend the broken leg of her short stool. She always sat on that stool when she mended my clothes, chopped up the yellow discarded vegetable leaves for our ducks or chickens, or smoked her water pipe.

"Maybe he is still in the backyard," Ah Pau said as she kept on fixing her stool.

I went to look for him. Kee might be able to help me. Even though he often bossed me, he was the person in the family besides Ah Pau who I felt closest to. I had followed him everywhere when I came to live with Ah Pau a few years ago. Now I found Kee in the backyard, making a slingshot for himself.

"Hey, Kee, can you lend me fourteen cents?"

"Fourteen cents! What for?" He didn't raise his head, but pushed back his thick hair. The hair flopped down again and almost covered his eyes.

"I want to try an apple." I didn't want to tell him the whole story. He had a big mouth, and I was afraid that he would tell everybody. I wanted Ah Pau's dream coming true to be a surprise.

He raised his head, exclaiming, "Are you crazy? Apples are rich people's fruit."

"But there is nothing written on the apples that says they belong only to rich people."

"Even if there isn't, can you afford to buy one?"

"An apple costs only sixteen cents."

"*Only* sixteen cents! That's enough to buy me three or four slingshots."

"I will give you one bite of the apple if you lend me the money."

"Uh-uh."

"Don't *you* want to try one?"

"Of course I'd like to try one, but I'll wait until I'm rich."

"I don't want to wait. I want to try one *right now!*"

"Too bad you weren't born into a rich family," Kee said. He tried to flip his hair back, but it was no use. It flopped down again at once. "You'd better get that silly idea out of your mind."

I didn't pay any attention to him but went next door to find Ah Mei. Maybe she could help me find a way to make money. She was always on my side. When I went into her house, she was doing her homework.

"Hey, I want to tell you a secret, Ah Mei, but you have to swear first."

"What secret?"

"Secret means secret! I want you to swear before I tell you."

So Ah Mei stuck up three fingers and swore, "On top of me is the heaven god, below me is the earth god, and I, Chan Mei, am in the middle. If I tell Ying's secret, I will be punished by the heaven god and the earth god!"

I lowered my voice, "I want to buy an apple."

She exclaimed, "You really mean it?"

"Of course."

"Are you sure you are all right?"

"Oh, come on, Ah Mei. I haven't told you the whole thing yet."

"What whole thing?"

"I want to give half an apple to my Ah Pau for her seventy-first birthday present."

"Whaah! But . . . how can you buy it?"

"That's why I came to ask you if you have any idea how I can make money."

"Why don't you think of another present instead of an expensive apple!"

"Never mind, Ah Mei."

"You might knit a scarf for her. . . ."

"I *hate* to knit. You know that."

I left Ah Mei's house with her saying, "You have a lot of choices!"

I went to our backyard to see Kee again, but he was not there. I sat down and leaned on the lichee tree in the middle of the backyard. I had planted the lichee tree when I first came to live here, but the tree had not produced any lichee nuts yet. I was very sad because I didn't know how to find ways to make money.

I wished Ah Pau's birthday would be later instead of only ten days from now. Maybe Kee and Ah Mei were right. Maybe I should give up and wait until I grew up and made money and was rich, then I could buy anything in the whole wide world for Ah Pau. But Ah Pau's long-time dream wouldn't become true even if

it had been sixty years. Sixty years! No. I couldn't give up just like that. I couldn't let Ah Pau wait any longer. I wanted Ah Pau's childhood dream to come true. She was always so good to me.

But how?

I scratched my head to think and think. Suddenly I heard Ah Pau calling me, "What are you doing in the backyard? Have you done your homework yet?"

"Coming!" I got up, ready to go. At the corner of my eye I spotted my basket of junk in the storage room.

"I've got it!" I said to myself.

CHAPTER 8

I dashed into the storage room to look at the junk that I had been collecting for a long, long time. There was only a small pile of white broken glass, a pair of rubber soles for shoes, and a small bag of duck feathers. I was very disappointed because I didn't think I would get fourteen cents from the junk man.

I looked at Kee's junk in another basket. He

had three times as much as I had! With my things plus his, maybe I *could* get fourteen cents. So I went back to look for Kee.

"Can I have your junk, Kee?" I found him upstairs in the study, mending his kite.

"No! I have been saving that for a long time."

"Then can I *borrow* it from you?"

"Why don't you save enough and then buy your apple?"

"I don't know how long it will take. Hey, if I tell you my secret, will you let me borrow your junk?" I couldn't worry about his big mouth anymore.

"I don't want to hear what kind of secret you have. It's always gossip. Why don't you just mind your own business?"

"I'm not gossiping this time. It's about Ah Pau."

"Grandma?"

I knew Kee was curious, and I jumped at the chance. "See, Ah Pau's seventy-first birthday is coming soon. I want to give her half an apple

for her birthday present. Can you let me have your junk now, since I told you my secret?"

I thought he might change his mind, but he still said no.

"Hey! I have an idea," I said. "Let's both get Ah Pau the apple. You pay half, I pay half." That was my last strategy. But I really didn't want to do it that way because then I couldn't have my half of the apple.

Kee stared at me for a few seconds. Then he declared, "I'd better wait till I get rich. Then I'll give her an expensive present."

"An apple *is* an expensive present."

"Of course, I'll give her something more expensive than your apple, dummy!"

"You just don't want to give her anything, that's all. You're stingy, stingy, stingy!" I sang louder and louder as I walked away, ready to go out to look for more junk on the street.

Suddenly Kee called out, "Hey! I'll make a deal with you!"

"What deal?"

"I'll let you have my junk, but you'll have to

loosen the dirt and pull the weeds for me in the pumpkin patch."

"But that's a lot of work."

"Do you want the junk or not?"

Kee's junk was my only hope. I knew that no matter how hard I looked for junk, there was no way I could get that much within ten days. I was so afraid that he would change his mind that I hurriedly answered him, "Yes! Yes!" Then I dashed toward the stairs.

"Not yet," Kee stated slowly. "You have to finish your job before I'll give the junk to you. It's only fair business."

"What if I can't finish before Ah Pau's birthday?"

"That's up to you. If you want the junk, you'll have to work for it."

Even though I knew it was a lot of work, I had to do it. "I'll finish it before Ah Pau's birthday," I promised.

"And one more thing . . . ," he added, sniffling.

"What's that?" I knew something bad was

coming because of the way he sniffled.

"You can't tell Ah Pau that you had to do the work for me. She would jump on me for taking advantage of you again."

"Oh, I won't."

"And. . . ." He sniffled again. "You'll have to pay me interest."

"What's that?"

"That means you'll have to pay me back more than I lent to you. It's just like people borrowing money from a bank."

"You mean I have to pay you back? You said you'd let me *have* the junk. I'm already doing your work in the pumpkin patch."

"You asked if you could *borrow* it, remember?"

"But . . ." I could hardly speak.

"Don't worry." He sniffled again. "I'm not asking you to pay back the interest right now. You can just wait until New Year's and give me all your *lai see* money."

That seemed better. I'd get at least fifteen or twenty cents *lai see* money at New Year's, and I didn't think Kee's junk would be worth that much.

"Yes or no?" Kee sure knew how to do business.

"Okay," I finally agreed. I didn't want to bargain with him. He might change his mind, and I would never be able to get my apple. "Let's seal the bargain," I said.

I was ready to hook his little finger with mine, but he said, "Who wants to do that silly girls' stuff?"

But I didn't listen to him. I just grabbed his little finger and hooked mine three times. Then I pulled out a hair and threw it in the air. I spit on the floor and said, "If you break the bargain, you have to find my hair and lick my spit!"

CHAPTER 9

*F*rom that day on, before I came home from school, I went to the Hing Kee fruit store with my fingers crossed to see if any apples were left. Then I returned home and hoped nobody would buy any apples before I did.

As soon as I got home from school at 3:30, I did my homework. It was always the same: ten word problems in math, two pages of calligraphy, ten questions in reading, or sometimes reciting a whole lesson by memory. I did it without my usual stalling.

Then I took a spade and a *chaam,* a crescent-shaped basket made of split bamboo, sneaked out the back door so Ah Pau wouldn't know, and went to Ford Hill. I didn't know if Ford Hill belonged to Chan Village or not, but almost every family in the village had one small garden patch on the hillside. Everyone planted pumpkins all the way to the top because pumpkins didn't require much watering.

At the foot of the hill, where Ah Pui's family had their garden, greens like *bok choi,* green onions, and mustard greens were planted. There was a large man-made hole close to Ah Pui's garden, which collected rain water. The green vegetables needed water at least once a day. Our patch was located almost on top of Ford Hill. Kee and I could run up there on the zigzag dirt path without stopping. Ah Pau had to stop several times before she could reach the top.

When I got there this time, I didn't climb up

in the lichee tree near our patch as I always did to see where the silver snakelike river would end up. I just went straight to work. I didn't mind that there was nobody on the hill or that the weeds had grown like crazy since it rained several days before. I didn't even mind that I had to be very cautious not to break the vines where there were small pumpkins. But I *was* afraid that there were snakes hiding underneath the big leaves!

Before I squatted down, I often used a stick to hit the rows to scare away the snakes. But I was still afraid that when I raised up a vine or the leaves, a snake would suddenly shoot up in the air. So I kept singing or saying classical poems or reciting my lessons as loud as I could to scare away the snakes while I pulled up the weeds. I couldn't work very long because it was the middle of September, and the sun went down early.

By the time I went home it was dark, and my back was aching. My voice was hoarse, and I was exhausted. But I didn't care. When I

thought about how sweet the apple would be, how surprised Ah Pau would be at my present, and how proud my uncle would be because I was the only one to make Ah Pau's childhood dream come true, then I didn't feel tired anymore. After a full night's sleep, I would be as energetic as before.

Finally, two days before Ah Pau's birthday, I finished the work in the pumpkin patch. I couldn't believe it!

Kee was wrong. He had thought that I couldn't finish the work on time. "Let me check and see," he said, and he went up the hill and checked. He couldn't find any fault, and he didn't want to find my hair and lick my spit. "You won this time," he said.

Unwillingly, he let me borrow his junk.

I dumped mine and his together into a *chaam*, the same one I used for the weeds. I could hardly wait to sell it to the junk man. The next day, right after school, I carried my junk on my shoulder from street to street, block to block, trying to find the junk man. I had to sell it. But I had been looking for three blocks, and I still didn't see the junk man. I prayed that he was not sick at home. . . .

What was that? I listened carefully. A bell ringing! It was *his* bell ringing! I followed the sound, turned into the fourth block, and heard the junk man shout, "High prices for junk!" I quickly picked up my pace and rushed toward the sound.

"Hey, Mr. Junk Man! Wait! I want to sell my stuff to you," I announced loudly.

The junk man heard me and turned around. He was carrying two big split-bamboo baskets on his shoulder with a bamboo pole. I hurried to reach him and lowered my *chaam* to the ground.

"What do you have, little girl?" he asked. He lowered his baskets to the ground, too.

"How much can I get for this junk?" I asked. I crossed my fingers, hoping that he would give me at least fourteen cents. I tried my best to convince him: "See, I have a real brass kettle, two rubber soles, and—"

He didn't listen to me. He just picked up Kee's funny little old vase and studied it for a couple of minutes. I held my breath, hoping he would buy everything. The more things he wanted, the more money I could get. But he didn't even look at the broken brass kettle to see if it was made of real brass. He didn't check the rubber soles or inspect the duck feathers to see if they were mixed with chicken feathers, which were of no use. He didn't check to see if the clear glass was mixed with colored glass, which he never bought. I had hoped that he would offer me fourteen cents so I would have enough money for one apple. But from the way he acted, I knew for sure that my dream was dead. I would never be able to buy an apple and give half to Ah Pau for her birthday. My hard work for Kee in the pumpkin patch had been for nothing. I was about to beg the junk man to buy my stuff when suddenly, very cautiously, he whispered, "I'll give you seventeen cents. Okay?"

"Seventeen cents?" I couldn't believe my

ears! That meant that I would get three cents extra! It was much more than I expected. I knew I could bargain with him for a little more. I had seen Kee bargain with him before. But I didn't want to. What if he changed his mind and decided not to take my stuff? Then I would get nothing. So I replied happily, "Okay."

He carefully wrapped the funny little old vase in his handkerchief and put it into his right pocket. Then he dumped the brass kettle and shoe soles into one basket, and the broken glass and the small bag of duck feathers into the other.

I didn't understand why he liked that little old vase so much, while he ignored the other things. It was just an old vase! He took a bundle of money from his left pocket and counted out exactly seventeen cents.

Wow! Kee would really regret that he loaned me his junk if he found out how much I had gotten from the junk man!

CHAPTER 10

I raced back home without stopping, threw the empty *chaam* in the backyard, then ran off to the Hing Kee fruit store before Ah Pau or Kee could spot me. There were still two apples. Although the apples did not look as red and shiny as before, they were still apples, and still attractive.

"I'm going to buy an apple," I said proudly to the owner.

"They cost sixteen cents." He didn't pay much attention to me. Instead, he went to wait on a man who was dressed very nicely, like a rich person.

I waited nervously, afraid that the well-dressed man would buy the apples before I could. If he did, I would die right in front of him! But he only bought two pieces of sugarcane and left. I wiped the sweat off my forehead. Before another customer could come, I told the owner, "I have seventeen cents. I want to buy an apple."

"Where's your money?"

"Here." I handed him sixteen cents.

He counted the money and put it into a pocket of the canvas apron that he wore. Then he asked, "Which apple do you want?"

"I want the one on the left." I had studied both apples carefully, and the one on the left seemed a tiny bit larger.

He picked up the apple on the left and asked, "Do you want me to cut it for you?"

I hesitated for a few seconds. Then I replied,

"Yes. Cut it with one side bigger than the other." I decided the bigger side would be for Ah Pau. With both hands, I took the apple carefully from him. It was heavy, cool, and it smelled good. It seemed like an unbelievable dream. I almost cried. At that moment, I decided to walk to Uncle's store to show him the apple before I gave it to Ah Pau. It was just about ten stores away.

As I was walking toward my uncle's store, I kept sniffing and sniffing the apple. Ummm . . . it smelled so good that I wished I could keep that smell forever and ever! I was amazed that the inside of the apple was nearly white! I had thought it would be red. Oh, what were these? Seeds? There were a couple of small, smooth brown things inside. They must be seeds. Hey! I can try to plant them. Maybe I'll have luck in growing them.

As I was wondering if I should try to plant them in the backyard next to my lichee tree or on top of Ford Hill next to our pumpkin patch, I heard a rough, mean voice over my shoulder.

"Where did you get the money?"

Oh, no, not again. I didn't need to turn around. I knew who it was. I held the apple tightly.

"You stole the money," Ng Shing said.

"Who says so? I did not!" I kept walking quickly.

"You're lying! I'm going to tell on you!"

"I don't care! I didn't steal it!"

He jumped in front of me, staring at my apple. "Give me half, and I won't tell on you."

"I won't!" I refused firmly.

"I'll tell the other kids you're not my girlfriend anymore if you give half to me," he bargained. I saw a sly smile on his face.

Mrs. Yu hadn't punished Ng Shing. She told *me* to ignore him, and I couldn't stop the boys in my class from calling me Shing's girlfriend. I hated it! And I couldn't get any help from Kee because lately he would lock himself in the storage room for hours, and he wouldn't let anyone go in. All I could hear were sounds of sawing and hammering.

Well, it would almost be worth it if Ng Shing agreed to stop, I thought. If I did what he told me to do, I could ask Ah Pau to give me a bite of her half, and I could still taste the apple. I asked, "Are you telling me the truth?"

"Sure."

"You swear?"

He raised up his right arm and swore rapidly, "On top of me is the heaven god; below me is the earth god. I, Ng Shing, am in the middle. If I lie to Yeung Ying, I will be punished by the heaven god and earth god."

Unwillingly, I handed the small half to him. He grabbed it greedily, but when he noticed that my half was bigger, he demanded, "No! I want *that* half!"

"No! That's for my Ah Pau!"

"*I* want it!"

"No! That's—" Before I could finish, he slapped my hand hard. Ah Pau's apple fell out of my hand and rolled into a storm drain, and Ng Shing ran away with the other half.

At once I dropped to the ground, trying to

get my apple from the drain. But my hand was too big to fit through the bars of the grate on the drain, and my arm was not long enough to reach around the bars into the drain. I couldn't reach my apple! I could only watch it sinking into the smelly, gooey mud. . . .

"You die, Ng Shing! I hope lightning strikes you!" I yelled and cried at the same time.

CHAPTER 11

With the apple gone, I didn't want to find anything else to substitute for Ah Pau's present. There was nothing better than half an apple. And I didn't want to mention it to her, to Kee, to Ah Mei, or to anyone. The hurt was deep, and talking about it would make me cry. I didn't want to cry on Ah Pau's big day. It was a special, happy occasion for Ah Pau to be seventy-one and still very healthy.

On her birthday I got up early, about 6:30, but everybody, even Uncle, had gotten up earlier. When I stepped into the living room, it was already lit with candles, oil lamps, and incense burning on the worship table. Ah Pau had already given thanks to Buddha for giving her seventy-one years. I greeted Ah Pau brightly, "Happy birthday, Ah Pau! I hope you are always healthy and live a thousand years!"

Ah Pau was in a very happy mood. She replied, "Oh, I hope your wish comes true!"

Kee came in from the outhouse. He also greeted Ah Pau, and with a mysterious smile he said, "Happy birthday, Grandma!"

Auntie and Ah So were busy taking bowls of *ju yok juk*, pork meatball porridge, to the table for everybody. They had gotten up before dawn to cook it. This was a special treat for Ah Pau's big day because we usually didn't have breakfast except during Chinese New Year. We all sat around the table with a kerosene lamp in the middle. I greeted them all before I ate the *juk* because I was the youngest in the family. "Ah

Pau, eat. Uncle, eat. Auntie, eat. Ah So, eat. Kee, eat." Kee also mumbled a greeting to everybody—except me because he was older than I. The *juk* was delicious, not tasteless like the plain rice *juk* we usually ate. I liked the pork meatballs the most because they were mixed with green onions and spices. I wished Ah Pau's birthday would be every day so I could have *ju yok juk* to eat each morning!

While we were eating the steaming hot *juk*, I noticed that Ah Pau was wearing something I hadn't seen before. I exclaimed, "Ah Pau! You have a new vest."

"Yes. Your auntie made it for me. I told all of you not to give me anything," Ah Pau complained, but I could tell she was happy.

"Just a little something," Auntie said, sipping her *juk* gracefully. Kee, sniffling from putting too much pepper on the *juk*, stuck the whole spoon into his mouth. He was already on his second bowl, while I was only about halfway through my first.

Uncle looked at the old clock on the wall

and announced, "Before Kee and Ying go to school, I want you all to see. . . ." He took out a red embroidered cloth purse from his pocket. With both hands to show his respect, he gave the purse to Ah Pau, who sat next to him. "This is for you, Mother. I wish you long life."

Ah Pau at once put down her spoon, anxiously opened the cloth purse, and at the same time complained, "I told all of you that you didn't need to give me anything." Inside the purse were two flat, transparent pieces of green jade shaped like doughnuts. Ah Pau wept as she took them out. "They must have cost a fortune!" she cried. Then she took off her old gold earrings that were round loops and asked Ah So to help her put a piece of jade on each loop.

I brought a small mirror to Ah Pau. She admired herself in the mirror and shook her head gently. The pieces of thin jade and the gold earrings created tinkling sounds. I sure wished Uncle would give me the same kind of jade when I got to be seventy-one years old. Ah

Pau still complained that Uncle shouldn't have spent that much money on her. Uncle and Auntie exchanged looks and smiled. They knew that Ah Pau really liked the present.

While Ah Pau was admiring herself in the mirror, Ah So spoke softly, as she always did. "I made this for you, Grandma. I hope your life is always as happy as it is right now."

Ah Pau was so pleased, she couldn't close her mouth! "You are all spoiling me now. I feel like a new bride in my old age!"

"Grandma . . ."

Nobody paid attention to what Kee was about to say because we all looked at Ah So tying a bandanna on Ah Pau's forehead. Ah Pau looked at herself again in the mirror and declared, "It fits perfectly: not too tight and not too loose. The vest and the bandanna can keep me warm the rest of my life."

Suddenly Kee cleared his throat and pointed to the corner where Ah Pau usually sat to do things when it got cold. "Look! Everyone look!"

We all looked in that direction. A newly made stool shone under the dim light.

"Who bought that?" Ah Pau asked curiously.

"I *made* it!" Kee announced proudly as he stuck out his chest.

"When did you make it?" I asked, hoping that Kee was telling a lie.

"What do you think I was doing in the storage room, huh?" Then he jumped up from the table and brought the stool to Ah Pau. "Here, Grandma, sit down and try it out."

Ah Pau sat down and exclaimed, "It's just what I need, Kee! It's much, much sturdier than the old one."

"I know. I saw you trying to mend the old one." I had never seen Kee look so proud before.

"You are so observant. When did you learn how to make a stool, Kee?" Ah Pau asked.

Kee looked at me and smiled. He answered proudly, "Just these last few days!"

That's all I could take. "You said you were going to wait until you got rich, and then you would get her a present!" I said jealously.

"I changed my mind. This present didn't cost me anything. Not even a cent! I found the materials on the carpenter's scrap pile."

I hadn't felt so bad when Uncle, Auntie, and Ah So gave Ah Pau a present. They were old—much older than me—and they could earn money. What really bothered me was that Kee had given Ah Pau a present, and I hadn't. I felt betrayed and completely left out. Ah Pau, Uncle, Auntie—everybody must have thought I was stingy.

As Ah Pau was testing the stool to see if it wobbled or not, I mumbled to her, "I was supposed to have something for you, too, but I—"

"Yeah!" Kee interrupted. "You ate it *all*, stingy!"

I pretended I didn't hear him as I tried hard to keep back the tears. I didn't want to cry on Ah Pau's big day. The tears would wash away the happiness and luck. But Kee kept barking, "Yeah! Stingy!"

"No, I didn't eat it!" I couldn't keep back

the tears any longer. I started to cry.

"So, where is it, huh? Stingy!"

"*Enough*, Kee!" Uncle ordered.

Ah Pau got up and put her arm around me and said, "I didn't expect you and Kee to give me a present. All I want is for you to be a good girl and study hard. That's the most valuable present you could ever give me. Do you understand?"

I didn't understand, and I didn't want to mention my apple, either. It hurt even more when I thought about it.

Ah Pau wiped my tears with her hand and said, "Finish your *juk* and get ready for school."

But I couldn't eat.

"The apple was delicious!" Ng Shing said as I stepped into the classroom. He probably didn't even know what happened to Ah Pau's half of the apple.

"I hope you get struck by lightning!" I shouted.

CHAPTER 12

I desperately wanted to give Ah Pau another apple, even if it was late. I needed to show Ah Pau and Kee that I was *not* stingy. I thought and thought, trying to figure out a way to make money besides collecting junk. But it seemed hopeless.

Several days later on a Sunday afternoon, after we played jump rope in the plaza, Ah Mei suggested, "Let's go to Tai Gai."

"No, I don't want to," I told her. I didn't want to see Hing Kee fruit store. It would remind me of my lost apple. "We can play around at school."

"Okay," Ah Mei agreed.

We strolled to our school. It was so quiet when we got there. At first we played in the school vegetable garden, which was at both sides of the school's main entrance. The left side of the entrance was connected to someone else's vegetable garden, but separated by a three-foot-high stone wall. The student garden was only assigned to students from fourth to sixth grades. Each patch was about five feet by five feet. Compared to Ah Man's and the others, Kee's *bok choi* looked yellow and half dead. The dirt on the patch looked hard and dry. I didn't know how long it had been since he watered it. While I was looking for a clay flower pot to get water in, Ah Mei called, "Hey, Ying! Look at me!"

Ah Mei was on top of the stone wall, stretching out both arms and balancing herself.

"I can do that, too!" I said. We had never climbed on the wall before.

I decided to look for the pot later, and skipped to the stone wall. While I was trying to boost myself up, I heard Ah Mei say, "Look! So many plantains in that garden!"

I looked. The garden next to our student garden was about fifty feet wide and a hundred feet long and fenced. Plantains were scattered wildly along the edge of the fence, while *bok choi*, lettuce, and green onions were growing neatly in rows. I had never seen plantains in a garden before. They usually grew wild on the dirt paths between the rice paddies. Because people picked them to use in Chinese herb medicine, you didn't see many plantains in one place. I wondered why the owner of the garden didn't pull them up. He must not want them, I figured. An idea flashed into my head at once: I could collect them and sell them to the drug-store, then I would have money to buy another apple!

"Let's go pull them up," I suggested to Ah

Mei. I didn't tell her that I wanted to buy another apple. I wanted to keep it a secret until I actually gave the apple to Ah Pau. Then Ah Mei couldn't accuse me of eating it as Kee had.

"But the plantains are in someone's garden!"

"That's okay. They grow wild. See! They are all growing along the fence, not in rows. I'm sure no one planted them that way. It's okay to take the plantains as long as we don't mess up the vegetables."

"Let's go," she agreed.

So we jumped down into the garden. The plantains were even healthier, bigger, and greener than they had seemed when we looked from the wall. The dirt was soft and crumbly, and we could pull out the whole plant, including the root, which was the most expensive part. We used one hand to pull up the plants, but we didn't have a basket to hold them. So I held up the front of my *tong cheong sam* and made a pocket. I stuck the plants into it with dirt and everything. Ah Mei saw me do that, and she did the same, even though she was worried about getting her clothes dirty.

"You can wash them when you get home," I reminded her. "We're getting rich!" We could buy not only one apple, but two, three, four, or even more! The plants we had now would have taken us at least three to four years to collect from the dirt path beside the rice paddies! Ah Pau could have one whole apple by herself! Ah Kee, Ah So, Auntie, and Uncle could eat one, too.

Suddenly I heard someone shout, "What are you doing in my garden?"

Ah Mei and I both looked up and saw a small lady in black clothes running toward us with a long bamboo pole. Without consulting each other, we dropped all the plantains and ran to the stone wall. After I climbed up and jumped back to the other side, I discovered that Ah Mei was still struggling on the wall, so I turned to help her. Before I could pull Ah Mei over, the lady hit me on top of the head. I got dizzy and nearly fell.

"Are you all — " Ah Mei started to ask.

"Run, Ah Mei!" I yelled, pulling her back over the wall as I spotted the lady's bamboo pole about to come down on Ah Mei's head. I thought that after Ah Mei jumped back to the school side and we were not in the garden anymore we would be safe. But the small woman acted like a mad dog and kept stabbing out at us with her bamboo pole.

"If I ever catch you!" she shouted at us as if she were going to kill us.

We started to run. We passed the teachers' office, dormitory, and cafeteria. I was afraid the teachers would hear the noise. Many teachers lived at school, since most of them came from other towns. They might still be preparing for their classes or grading papers. They might hear the lady's shouts and come out to see what was going on. But we didn't have any choice because the lady was running fast and the pole was just above our heads.

After we passed the fifth- and sixth-grade classrooms, we ran across the lower-grade playground. The lady would not give up. We had to enter the long classroom building at the other end of the playground. There were six or seven first- and second-grade classrooms that ran along one side of the corridor. I was running faster than Ah Mei was. I knew that we needed to trick the lady; otherwise, she might chase us all the way home!

I gasped, "Hide! Hide!" as I entered the second classroom and slipped behind the door. Ah Mei dashed in and hid beside me. We both tried to catch our breath as we waited. We could still hear the lady shouting. We knew that she would not give up and go back. In a few seconds we heard her rapid footsteps in the corridor. Ah Mei and I peered through the crack between the door and the wall, afraid to breathe. I could hear my own heart beating noisily in my chest and eardrums. I hoped the lady couldn't hear the noises my body was making.

There she was! Through the crack we glimpsed a small, middle-aged lady with faded black clothes. She could really run, and she was still shouting, "If I ever catch you!"

After her voice faded a little and we knew she had passed our hideout, Ah Mei whispered, "Let's go."

"Wait." I stopped her, warning, "She'll return soon."

We waited. I could breathe more easily by then, but my mouth was so dry I could hardly swallow. I was right! The small lady finally returned. She still threatened, "I'll turn you in to the principal if I ever catch you!"

"What should we do?" We both looked at each other, terrified. It would really mean trouble if she did.

We waited and made sure that we couldn't hear her anymore. I tiptoed out to search in the direction she had gone and didn't see her, so I motioned Ah Mei to come out.

"That side?" Ah Mei whispered, because I wanted both of us to go out from the other side of the classroom building, not the side we had just come in.

"Yes. What if she is reporting us to the principal? We'd just be turning ourselves in."

"What if she really *does* report to him?"

"She doesn't know our names. That's why we'd better get out this way."

Ah Mei hesitated to go out the other exit. About five hundred feet from the end of the classroom building was a narrow dirt path on top of a dam that separated a pond from the river. Last year part of the dirt dam caved in, and the school had not allowed any of us to use it because the place that was broken had filled with water. Kids might fall in and drown by jumping over the broken gap.

But we had no choice. The main entrance to the school grounds was next to the lady's vegetable garden, and we would have to pass the teachers' office to get there, too. Even if the lady had not reported us to the teachers or the principal, she might be standing on the road in front of her garden at the school entrance, waiting for us to come out.

So we had to take a risk. We carefully walked along the narrow path. My legs felt shaky when

I saw the water rushing by below. Ah Mei, who was usually not as brave as I, easily jumped over the two-foot gap to the other side of the path. Then she called to me and said, "It's not that bad. It's not that bad!"

But I just couldn't do it. My legs wouldn't listen to me when I told them to jump. What if I fall? I kept worrying. There were no other people around. This place was far from the street and the teachers' office. If something happened to me, even if Ah Mei screamed at the top of her lungs, no one would hear her.

"Come on. It isn't as scary as you think," Ah Mei said.

After hesitating for a long time, I finally jumped safely over the water to the other side.

Ah Mei relaxed. She said, "I'm glad it's over."

"I don't know," I replied.

Ah Mei gave me a strange look and questioned, "Why do you say that? She doesn't know our names, does she?"

"She may *not* know. But I just don't want to

mention it anymore. Please don't tell anybody about this, especially my Ah Pau. Okay?"

"I won't. How's your head?"

When she reminded me, I massaged my head. It was still sore. "I'm okay," I said. "But my legs are still shaking. Let's get out of here."

CHAPTER 13

"*H*elp! Help!" Someone was chasing me and trying to hit me with an iron pole. But I couldn't run fast, and the iron pole was about to reach me.

While I was struggling to run fast, I heard a familiar voice. "You are all right. You are all right." It was Ah Pau. She embraced me, but I could feel my heart throbbing hard. Ah Pau gave me a cup of cold tea to calm me down. She comforted me and said, "It was just a bad dream. Everything is all right."

But everything was *not* all right. I felt miserable, and I had lost my appetite. Ah Pau was worried. Hoping I would eat, she fixed me a cut-up bass fish head steamed with ginger and green onions, one of my favorite foods and something that Kee and I always fought over. But I only ate a little bit. It didn't taste as good as usual.

Kee was glad I didn't feel like eating. He quickly moved my dish in front of him and declared, "Good! Now *I* can eat it!"

But Ah Pau was worried. She put her hand on my forehead to see if I had any fever and said, "Your head is as cool as a cucumber. I don't know why you don't want to eat."

Auntie suggested, "Perhaps she is worried about her schoolwork."

"Are midterm exams coming soon?" Ah Pau asked. Her eyes had not left me.

"Not yet," I said. I was ashamed of what was bothering me.

To tell the truth, I wished I did have a fever. I wished I were as sick as the time I had chicken pox, so I wouldn't have to go to school. I was afraid to use the main entrance to school. I worried that the lady would be standing in front of her garden next to the school entrance, trying to find out who had stolen her plantains.

So I began to get up earlier and slip out of the house before Ah Pau could have a chance to ask me why. I sneaked into the school by jumping over the forbidden broken path before anybody could spot me. I hung around at school and waited until everybody had gone home. Then I jumped over the broken path and went home. That way, no one would see me and report to Mrs. Yu that I was breaking the school rule. Ah Pau questioned, "Why did you come home so late? Did you have detention?" But I didn't answer her. I pretended to concentrate on my homework.

Ah Mei, who was braver than I this time, walked right in and out of the entrance openly, as if nothing had happened.

At school, I always felt as though someone were searching for us among the students on the playground. I wanted to stay inside the class, but all the students had to be out during the ten-minute break after each period. So I hid in the bathroom during breaks. Every minute of class, I was scared that Mrs. Yu would ask us, "Who tried to steal plantains a few days ago?" I was afraid to look at her when she was teaching, afraid her eyes would see straight through me and discover my secret. Then she would point to me and command, "You, Yeung Ying, you thief, stand up!" It would be much, much worse than Ng Shing's saying that I was his girlfriend, even though he did announce to the class that I was no longer his girl. He was afraid the heaven god and earth god would punish him if he didn't.

I couldn't stand it anymore. One day I went to see Ah Mei after school and whispered, "I think we should tell the lady what we did."

"Why? She doesn't know our names. She didn't recognize us, did she?"

"She didn't, but I'm scared."

"Scared of what? We didn't mean to steal. We thought the plantains just grew wild like others do. . . ."

"But I'll never feel right unless I explain to her."

"What if she turns you in to the principal? Then he will announce it to the whole school during assembly on Monday morning!"

"Oh, yeah." I chickened out. I didn't want the whole school to know that I was a thief, a plantain thief. . . . But I didn't know what else to do.

CHAPTER 14

*T*he next day, I was afraid to look directly into Mrs. Yu's eyes when she was lecturing. My mind was not on the book, but was far, far away. Suddenly Ng Shing elbowed me. "Stand up, dummy!"

I didn't know what was going on until I heard Mrs. Yu command, "Yeung Ying!"

Oh, no! I knew it would happen. I looked around and searched for help, even from Ng

Shing, but no one helped me. They were all waiting. I didn't have any choice but to stand up. I was trembling and felt very weak. My hands were wet. I wished a hole would open up where I was standing so I could hide in it. Mrs. Yu had finally discovered my secret. She was going to punish me, either send me to the principal or inform my Ah Pau. Ah Pau would be very upset and disappointed because I was the one who disgraced my family by being a thief. . . .

I just stood there, helplessly, until Mrs. Yu commanded, "Read!" I didn't know what she was talking about until she questioned me. "What's wrong, Yeung Ying? You haven't opened your book."

"I . . ."

"Concentrate. If I ever catch you daydreaming again, you'll have to write 'I have to pay attention in class' one hundred times. Do you understand?"

"Yes, Mrs. Yu."

"Now, open your book and read Lesson Six."

I could hardly wait for the break. When it came, I asked Ah Mei to go with me to the bathroom. I told her, "I can't stand this anymore. Will you go with me to apologize?"

"I'm afraid to. . . ."

"If you don't go, I'll go by myself."

"You mean it?"

"Yes."

"When are you going?"

"As soon as school is out."

"Well . . . are you going to turn *me* in, too?"

"No, you have to go yourself."

"Oh, thanks." She was very pleased. Then she said, "The lady really doesn't know who did it."

"You don't understand how I feel, Ah Mei."

After school I went straight to the small lady's house beside the vegetable garden. There she was, shining a brass cooking pot under a banyan tree in the front yard. Suddenly I lost my nerve. I wanted to retreat, but the lady had spotted me. She stood up and shouted, "Hey!

What are you doing here?"

"I—" I couldn't retreat, so I walked closer to her. "I—"

"Hey! Come out with it!" She obviously didn't recognize me at all.

"I . . . I came here . . . to apologize. . . . "

She looked me over carefully.

"I . . . was the one you chased several days ago." I lowered my head, ashamed of myself.

"Ah." Suddenly she seized my arm and yelled toward the door where there was a small faded sign: *Doctor Tam's Herbal Clinic.* "Doctor Tam! I caught her! I caught the little thief!"

At once I regretted going there. I should have listened to Ah Mei, I thought. By then, an old man with a long silver beard reaching to his chest hobbled to the door with a walking cane. The lady pushed me in front of him and said, "That's the little thief, Doctor Tam. If you don't punish her right now while she's young, she'll end up stealing gold later."

"Are you sure she's the one?" he asked, pointing at me with his walking cane.

She looked at me proudly and reported, "Yes, Doctor Tam. She came here and said so herself."

"She did?" Doctor Tam looked at me and told the lady, who must have been his servant, "Let her go."

"Yes, Doctor Tam." Unwillingly the lady released me, then went inside and brought a bamboo chair to Doctor Tam, who sat down clumsily. "You came here all by yourself?"

"Yes, Doctor Tam. I came here to apologize." I was not as frightened as before because he didn't look as angry as the small lady did.

"Did your mama tell you to come here?"

"No, Doctor Tam. Nobody told me to."

"You were not afraid you would be caught?"

He looked as if he were joking with me, but I was not sure. "I—" I cleared my throat and said, "I wanted to tell you that I didn't mean to steal your plantains. We thought all the plantains were growing wild, and that you didn't want them."

"Hmmm . . ." Doctor Tam stroked his beard

and stated slowly, "Did you know that coming onto my property without permission is considered trespassing?"

Oh, no. My mouth felt very dry. I had committed one more crime that I didn't even know about! I couldn't answer him. All the time I was thinking that picking someone else's stuff was stealing, but I had never thought about trespassing. . . . I had committed two crimes. He's going to turn me in to the principal for sure. I should have listened to Ah Mei.

"Did you know that?"

"No, sir . . . I . . . " I cleared my throat again. "I never thought about trespassing until now. All I thought about was the plantains, nothing else. Please believe me."

"I *do* believe you. From now on, please think at least twice before you do something."

"Yes, sir."

"Good. By the way, where's your friend?"

Uh-oh. He's going to turn in Ah Mei, too. Ah Mei could not get away, either. I defended her hurriedly. "She's a very good student. She's always number one in the class. It was *my* idea to pull the plantains."

"Why didn't *she* come with you?"

Will he send the lady to catch Ah Mei? I was sweating for Ah Mei. "She . . . she was afraid."

"Afraid of what?"

"Afraid you would punish her."

"Oh, well, tell her she doesn't need to be afraid. Tell her I forgive her."

"Oh, thank you, sir. Do you forgive *me*, too?"

"Of course."

"That means . . . that means you will not turn me in to the principal?"

"Oh, no. That's between you and me."

"Oh, thank you, Doctor Tam." I almost cried.

"You can go home now. Your mama will be worried about you."

"Thank you, thank you, Doctor Tam," I said, feeling as light as a feather. I bowed respectfully to him and turned, but he called me back.

"What is your name?"

"Yeung Ying."

"You live at Yeung Village?"

"No. I live in Chan Village with Ah Pau and her family. I am the only one named Yeung there."

Doctor Tam stroked his beard again. "I am very curious. Could you tell me, what did you plan to do with my plantains?"

"I . . . I planned to sell them to the drugstore."

"To buy candy?"

"No, I planned to buy another apple." Then I told him the whole story of my apple. It was the first time I had told anybody.

"You're a very nice little girl. Here." He took some money from his *tong cheong sam* pocket. "Go get another one."

"Oh, no!" I was surprised. "I couldn't take someone's money for nothing. But I appreciate your offering it, anyway."

"I don't blame you. If I had a granddaughter, I wouldn't like it if she took someone's money for nothing. Hmm, how about working for me for seven days to earn it?"

"How?"

"My servant will be out of town for a few days next month. Why don't you water the garden for me while she is gone?"

"Okay! I have a lot of experience doing that."

"Good! Here, take the money and go buy an apple so your birthday present won't be too late."

"Thank you, Doctor Tam." Without looking back, I raced to Hing Kee store. But there was not an apple in sight!

I was so disappointed. I asked the owner, who didn't chase me away this time, "Do you have any more apples?"

"No, no more."

"Are you going to get more?"

"Next year, not now."

"Oh . . . " I wanted to return the money to Doctor Tam right away, but I was afraid that Ah Pau would worry about me. So I hurried home and planned to return the money the next day.

The next morning Doctor Tam was taking his morning walk around his front yard.

"Good morning," he said, smiling. "How did the apple taste?"

"I didn't taste it. They sold all the apples. I came here to return your money."

"Oh? That's too bad. You were a little late, weren't you? Did you ask the owner if he would be getting any more apples?"

"Yes, I did. He said he would order some next year, but not now. Maybe Ah Pau and I can try one next year." I didn't feel nearly as disappointed as I had when I just found out that all the apples had been sold. At least I had accomplished one thing. Before I said good-bye to him, I looked over at the school entrance and said happily, "Do you know what, Doctor Tam? I can walk by the entrance freely again."

"What do you mean?" he asked, looking puzzled.

"I was afraid to walk by here before I apologized to you. Now I can walk by here a thousand times and not be afraid that your servant will catch me!"

CHAPTER 15

A week later, when I came home from school, Ah Pau was waiting for me at the door. Her face was bright with joy. "You must have met a distinguished person! Look what is on the table!"

I ran inside quickly and exclaimed, "An apple! Where did you get that apple?" It was a big red apple—bigger and redder and shinier than the ones I had seen at Hing Kee store.

"It's yours! A lady brought it here along with a note. She said her master had sent her here. Look and see what the note says."

I picked up the note lying beside the apple. It was written with a brush and ink. The characters looked shaky, as if the note were written by an old person. "Special order to a girl who has the courage to admit her mistakes. From an admirer."

"What mistakes?" Ah Pau asked.

"Don't ask me now, Ah Pau. Let's try it first!" I was ready to go to the kitchen, but I remembered something. "Oh, wait! Ah Pau, hold it." I put the apple into Ah Pau's hand. "See how heavy it is?"

Ah Pau held it. She weighed it in her hand and said, "It sure is heavy for its size."

"And it feels cool, too, see?" I put the apple on the back of her hand.

"It sure does."

"And wait, Ah Pau!" I ran to the kitchen and put the apple on the chopping board. With the cleaver, I carefully cut the apple, making sure that one side was bigger than the other. Then I used both hands to present the bigger half to Ah Pau and declared, "I hope you don't mind your birthday present being late."

"For my birthday!" Ah Pau cried. "Ah Pau has dreamed of eating an apple since your age." I saw tears rolling down her cheeks.

I burst into tears, too. I was overjoyed because I was the one to make Ah Pau's childhood dream come true at last. "Bite it, Ah Pau."

Ah Pau was about to bite her apple, but I stopped her. "Wait." Instead, I put my half of the apple in front of her nose. "Smell it, Ah Pau. Doesn't it smell good?"

Ah Pau sniffed it a couple of times and said, "Yes, it has a good smell."

We put the apples to our teeth. Ah Pau seemed to be having a difficult time because she had lost her two front teeth. She wanted to cut the apple into small pieces, but I insisted, "No. You have to *bite* it, Ah Pau. Our schoolbook said it's sweet and crunchy. You're sup-

posed to bite it so you can hear the crunchy sound it makes."

So she bit it carefully with her side teeth.

I bit mine. It was crunchy, but its crunch was not the same as sugarcane. It was sweet, but the sweetness was not the same as mango or papaya. It had its own special sweetness and crunch!

About that time Kee walked in and asked us, surprised, "What is it? An apple?"

"Yes. Want a bite?" I offered. But he shook his head proudly. "No, I can try it when I get rich."

"I hope you don't need to wait sixty years as I did, Kee!" Ah Pau commented, chewing her apple clumsily but with satisfaction.

About five minutes later Kee couldn't stand it and asked, without raising his head, "What does an apple taste like, anyway?"

"It's sweet and crunchy!" Ah Pau and I replied together.

Glossary

bok choi — A green, leafy Chinese vegetable used in stir-frying or to make soup.

catty — A unit of measurement equal to approximately one and one-third pounds.

chaam — A crescent-shaped basket made of split bamboo.

Chinese New Year — The Chinese use a lunar calendar in which New Year's Day usually occurs in January or February.

lai see — Money put into a red paper pocket, given to the younger generation by married relatives on birthdays or during Chinese New Year.

lichee tree — A tree that produces numerous fruit about the size of Ping-Pong balls, with a rough, reddish skin. Inside is a white, sweet, juicy pulp around a brown seed.

plantain — A weed with leaves at the base of the stem and tiny greenish flowers, used in Chinese herbal medicine.

tong cheong sam — Traditional Chinese tunic. The man's *tong cheong sam* buttons down the front, similar to a Kung Fu outfit, while the woman's buttons down the right side.